DO YOU ENJOY BEING FRIGHTENED?

**WOULD YOU RATHER HAVE
NIGHTMARES
INSTEAD OF SWEET DREAMS?**

**ARE YOU HAPPY ONLY WHEN
SHAKING WITH FEAR?**

CONGRATULATIONS ! ! ! !

YOU'VE MADE A WISE CHOICE.

**THIS BOOK IS THE DOORWAY
TO ALL THAT MAY FRIGHTEN YOU.**

GET READY FOR

COLD, CLAMMY SHIVERS

RUNNING UP AND ▓▓▓▓▓▓▓▓▓▓▓E!

**NOW, OPEN▓▓▓
IF YOU ▓▓▓E !!!!**

Shivers

THE LOCKED ROOM

M. D. Spenser

Plantation, Florida

ISBN 1-57657-049-5

EXCLUSIVE DISTRIBUTION BY PARADISE PRESS, INC.

Cover Design by George Paturzo
Cover Illustration by Eddie Roseboom

Printed in the U.S.A.

To Christian

<u>Chapter One</u>

I was getting a little tired of feeling sorry for everybody else.

My little brother, for instance. He looked nervous. He chews his lip when he's worried, which leaves a bright red rash under his mouth. Very attractive.

Mom just looked tired. Whenever she caught me looking at her, she gave me this big cheerful smile. Yeah right, Mom.

You're happy, I'm happy, the whole family's happy. Moving is just a big adventure. It's important to try new things. And Bill — The Stepfather — is just the best.

Moving is a lot of work. Especially when you've lived in a house for eleven years, which is my whole life. We had stuff crammed everywhere. When we had our yard sale, Mom made $1,356.12!

Have you ever actually *seen* that much money?

After the yard sale, Mom and I spread the money out on the living room rug and counted. I sorted the dollar bills into towers, while she tackled the mountains of change. Eric danced around with bare feet, nickels sticking out between his toes.

I figured that was the most fun I'd have for a long time.

Not that I wasn't excited. I mean, California just *sounded* exciting. I enjoyed telling people we were moving there. They always looked jealous.

Of course, I didn't mention where we were going in California.

Podunksville. A little brown town in the middle of nowhere.

The only good thing about the place was that my mom was born there. Her brother and sister, my Uncle Ian and Aunt Bonnie, still lived just outside of town. Aunt Bonnie lived in the farmhouse where all three of them grew up, and Uncle Ian lived in a trailer just down from the house.

I planned to spend as much time at the farmhouse as I possibly could.

Anything to get away from *him*. Watching *him* and Mom together was still hard.

I really couldn't explain why I didn't like my new stepfather. He'd been real nice to us. He paid lots of attention to my mom. He was even kind of handsome, especially compared to my dad.

My dad was going bald, while the Stepfather

had thick black hair. My dad had wrinkles. The Stepfather's skin was smooth.

My dad had a gap between his front teeth. Naturally, the Stepfather had a terrific smile.

Thinking about Dad made me want to look at him. I pulled my locket out of my T-shirt, and popped it open with my thumb. There was Dad's picture on the right, Mom's on the left — both of them fresh from college, soon to marry.

Eric leaned across the aisle.

"Can I see?" he asked wistfully.

"Give it right back," I said.

Mom glanced up from her magazine and frowned as she saw the locket exchanging hands.

"You two start to get your things together. We're going to be landing soon," she murmured.

"Mom, when is Dad going to visit us in California?" asked Eric, staring at the pictures in the locket.

"I don't know, Sweetie. It's expensive to fly here from the East Coast. I'm sure he'll be out just as soon as he can afford a ticket. He's going to miss you both like crazy."

"I want him to come out now," Eric whined. "I miss him."

"Well, you can call him tonight."

Mom reached over, squeezed Eric's hand, and smiled at both of us.

"I know you're both going to be homesick at first — for your friends and your dad and all the familiar things we've left behind. But please remember that Bill is very fond of both of you. We're going to have a wonderful life out here. It'll just take time."

"Is Bill going to be at the airport?" I asked.

"Yes, honey. We'll get our suitcases and drive straight to the house."

"Tell me again what my new room looks like," I said.

Mom laughed a little to herself.

"Well, it's really a very pretty room," she said, "although the rose wallpaper takes some getting used to. The room's got two dormer windows that look out over the front yard. Each dormer has a sweet little door on one side, like a cupboard door, where you can put toys and stuff."

"How big are the cupboards? Like, could I fit in them?" asked Eric.

"I guess you could," Mom said doubtfully. "I'm not sure how safe the flooring is. They're dark inside. I didn't really see how big they are."

"They sound cool, like a secret hideout," I said. "I'm going to put a flashlight and my sleeping bag in one. I might even sleep in there."

"We'll see. I'm not sure if I should tell you this yet, but I talked with Bill last night about the possibility of redecorating your room. You know, maybe changing the rug and painting the walls a different color. He said he'd think about it. If Bill says it's OK, you might have fun picking out your own colors and curtains."

I turned my head to hide my smile. I didn't want her to think I liked anything about this move, or about her marrying again, or about Bill. Bill Beard.

Beard. What a stupid last name.

Chapter Two

A sugary voice interrupted my thoughts.

"Ladies and gentlemen, the captain has posted the 'fasten seat belt' sign in preparation for landing. Please return all seats and tray tables to their upright position. All electronic devices and personal computers should be turned off at this time."

I straightened my seat and folded up my tray, and jammed the crumpled napkin into my cup. The stewardess was coming down the aisle with a trash bag.

"Give it back, Eric," I said, reaching across the aisle for my locket.

"Just a minute," he said, holding it away while he pretended to study the faces inside.

"*Now*, Eric," I said a little louder. "You're being the biggest jerk in the whole wide world. Now give it."

"I'll give it back if you'll let me sleep in the secret hideouts."

"You won't need to sleep . . . because you'll be

dead if you don't give me the locket this instant," I threatened.

Mom looked up.

"Brittany, I don't like your language," she said. "What's the problem?"

"No problem, Mom," Eric said. "I'm just giving Britt her locket."

With that, the little brat leaned across his arm-rest, the necklace dangling from his fingers, and looking me straight in the eyes — dropped my locket right into the stewardess's trash bag!

I actually heard the stewardess say "thank you." I reached backwards and yanked the bag away from her.

I scrabbled around in the bottom of the bag frantically, while the stewardess watched, my brother giggled, and my mother said "Brittany!" about twenty times.

Finally, I tilted the bag slightly, and felt the necklace slither to the bottom corner. I reached in with my eyes closed and pulled out the soda-soaked chain.

"Thank you," I said lamely to the stewardess, as I handed her the bag.

"Fasten your seat belt," she said rudely.

Eric and I turned to watch as her blue-clad form stalked down the aisle. For the thousandth time, I vowed never to speak to my brother again.

Mom made sure that wasn't an option, at least for the next hour. Eric and I weren't allowed to talk, period, until we got to the new house.

Everything was so unfair — moving to a new place with no friends, a whole new school to get used to, and a stepfather I could never like.

And on top of everything else, an eight year old brother who has dedicated his life to making me look stupid, and a mother who couldn't care less.

I dried my locket with the used napkin. I opened it again to look at Dad's face. My eyes filled up again. At least Dad used to listen to my side of the story.

I started to close the locket slowly.

Out of the corner of my eye, I saw my Mom's tiny portrait shift slightly. I blinked, squinting away my tears.

Slowly, I opened the locket all the way.

Mom's face seemed to dim, and then brighten. But now it wasn't Mom.

The hair was too dark. And the eyes of this woman were hollow and so *sad.*

The face in the locket looked at me in horror. The woman's eyes widened. Her mouth opened.

And then a thin razor-red line appeared across her throat!

Chapter Three

"Mom!" I gasped.

The necklace fell to the floor. I hit my head on the seat in front of me as I snatched it up.

Frantic, I stared at her image, bringing the locket an inch away from my eyes. My hands were shaking so hard I couldn't focus.

I couldn't believe what I saw.

The pictures were totally normal. Both were exactly as they'd always been. Color photographs of Mom and Dad — yearbook-style head shots.

Nothing like this had ever happened to me before. I opened and closed the locket several times. Normal, totally normal.

I shook my head, suddenly aware of sounds around me. The plane was descending. I popped my ears, wondering. Was that maniacal laughter mixed with the roar of the engines?

Maybe the change in cabin pressure was affecting my brain.

Then I glanced across the aisle. Eric was killing himself laughing. He'd caught the whole dropping-of-the-locket, hitting-of-the-head routine.

I felt my face turn red. I jerked my head around and stared out the window. I heard Mom tell Eric that he had just added thirty more minutes of silence to his time. Well, that was something.

I stole another glance at the pictures in the locket. Totally normal. What was my problem?

During the next hour, I was actually glad that Eric and I weren't allowed to talk.

Bill was waiting for us at the gate. I carried my backpack and a bag so I didn't have to shake hands or hug him or anything. We picked up our suitcases at baggage claim and struggled to the car.

Mom and Bill had lots to talk about during the drive.

I concentrated on the back of Bill's head. His hair was so black it was almost blue.

I suspected that Bill read books on how to be a good stepfather.

Knowing this is a difficult time, a good stepfather doesn't force conversation. A good stepfather catches your eye in the rearview mirror and smiles. A good stepfather gives your mother a light kiss at the airport, nothing passionate. A good stepfather hears that the children are not allowed to speak, and just

10

shakes his head ruefully.

I settled down as we drove. Whatever had happened on the plane seemed a lot less real in the bright sunshine, with trees and fields flashing by.

Plus, I was looking for my favorite fast food restaurants, the video store, the ice cream stand, the donut shop — and, of course, the mall.

Mile after mile went by, and I didn't see any of these things.

Eric broke the silence.

"Mom, can we talk now? Please?"

"I suppose so," Mom replied.

I rolled my eyes. So much for his extra thirty minutes.

"When are we going to get there?" Eric asked.

Bill looked over his shoulder, smiling.

"Just fifteen more minutes, son," he said. "Almost there. Hey, look, cows!"

"Cows!" I screamed sarcastically. "I never *saw* cows before!"

Mom turned to glare at me. She mouthed the words "don't you dare."

"Uh, Bill," I said in a normal voice, "are there any stores near your house, or places to eat? All I see are farms and fields. And, like, where's the school?"

"Good questions," said Bill. "My house is about ten miles outside of town. You and Eric will have to ride buses to school. And the mall is on the south side of town, much closer to where your aunt and uncle live. I'm afraid my house — uh, *our* house — is kind of in the middle of nowhere."

"But it's beautiful out there," Mom said. "I think you two will love living in the country."

"Here's our turn," said Bill. "We leave the highway, go about six miles down this road, and my driveway's on the left."

"Are there any kids in the neighborhood?" Eric asked in a quavery voice.

"I've never seen any," said Bill, "but if there are, I'm sure you and Brittany will find them."

Eric and I looked at each other with dismay.

No kids! Middle of nowhere! No signs of civilization! Where was Mom taking us? Eric and I looked silently out our windows, until the car slowed and veered left.

We stared down a dirt road lined with trees. A gray two-story house with wide porch and brooding windows waited for us at the end of the drive. I heard Eric take a deep breath.

As the car wound its way towards the house, a flock of crows rose like black flags before us.

Chapter Four

"Oh Bill, it's even prettier than I remembered!" Mom exclaimed. "You've put flowers in!"

"They do look nice, don't they? I forget what they're called: uh, beg — begone — "

"Begonias!" Mom laughed. She spoke to us over her shoulder as the car stopped in front of the house. "Bill's not the gardening type, kids. But I'm hoping you guys will help me plant lots of flowers. This old house needs some color. And I want to try a vegetable garden."

We each got out of the car and stretched while we looked around. I felt wobbly and wondered what Eric was thinking. A little song played in my head — "This is IT, this is IT" — and I clutched my locket for support.

The house looked real old, as if it had always been there. I liked the porch, which ran across the whole front of the house. It was supported by six vine-covered columns, two of which framed the front door.

A large gable jutted over the front door. A fan-

13

shaped window was set in the center. I pointed to it.

"Mom, is that my room?" I asked hopefully.

"No, honey. Your room's there, with those two dormer windows." She pointed to the left of the gable. "And those two dormers on the right are in the master bedroom, where Bill and I sleep. Eric, honey, your room looks out over the backyard."

Bill put his arm over Mom's shoulders.

"Let's leave the stuff in the car, and give the kids the tour," he said. "We can unpack later."

Mom held out a hand to Eric and we walked up the front steps. I stayed a little behind the group.

The house seemed huge inside. We stepped into a shady green entryway. The stairwell loomed before us, six stairs up, then a curved landing, and — I assumed — more stairs beyond that. A stretch of hallway ran alongside the stairs and disappeared into a darker part of the house. Several rooms appeared to lead off the hall.

We looked in each, and I counted them off with amazement: the "parlor" (I didn't know there was such a thing anymore), the library, and the spare room with guest bed. One door was a hall closet for coats, and another opened to reveal narrow stairs to the basement.

"I'm afraid the house needs a woman's touch," Bill said. "I stay so busy with work and traveling that I tend to live just in the kitchen, which has been modernized a bit. Otherwise, the house is pretty much as it's always been."

Mom interrupted.

"Bill grew up in this house, kids," she said. "His family has owned it for several generations."

"How old is it?" I asked.

"The original house was built in 1862 by the first William Beard," Bill said. "That small house — a cabin, really — burned down. This house was built the following year."

"How did it burn down?" Eric asked.

Bill smiled tightly, glancing at Mom.

"Well, that's not the most pleasant story..." He said, pausing.

Mom nodded permission.

"The first William Beard came to this part of the world because of the California Gold Rush," Bill continued. "He was one of the lucky few to actually find a substantial vein of gold — "

"Near here?" Eric blurted.

Bill leaned against the wall.

"No, no — north of here, several hours away. He came here to purchase land for farming and to build a grand house, worthy of the beautiful young bride he brought with him. He adored her. Unfortunately, she did not return his feelings, though she pretended to."

Bill paused.

15

"Now, remember, those were dangerous times. Gold fever made a lot of people greedy, and guns were like umbrellas — everybody had one. William Beard kept his money in a special box made of steel. The box could only be opened by one key, and he kept that key on him at all times."

"Even when he took a shower?" asked Eric.

Mom laughed.

"They took baths in those days, honey," she said. "And very few of those."

"Actually," Bill continued, "he wore the key on a chain around his neck — when he bathed, and ate, and slept. He only took the key off once, after his young wife begged and insisted for days. She claimed she wanted to wear it, close to her heart, for just one night. Foolishly, he believed her. That night she rose from the bed, robbed him blind, and fled into the darkness. But first she set the cabin on fire, hoping to destroy the evidence of her crime."

"So he died in the fire?" I asked. There's no way I'm going to be able to sleep in *this* house, I thought.

"No," said Bill. "Thankfully, William woke up before the flames spread to the bedroom. For one dreadful moment, he feared his wife was in the other room, trapped by flames. But then he saw the steel box, open and empty, dragged out from under the bed, and he knew instantly what had happened. The key was still in the lock. He grabbed the box and escaped out the window."

"What happened to the wife?" I wondered.

"They never found her," Bill said coldly. "And William never spoke of her again. He was a very clever man, and was able to rebuild a portion of his earlier fortune."

"It's amazing that you know so much about your family history," Mom marveled. "It's as if you were there."

Bill's face reddened.

"Believe me, I've heard the story so often, I could recite it in my sleep," he said. I hope I didn't bore you . . . heh, heh."

He cleared his throat abruptly and led them into the kitchen.

I looked around with relief. This room, at least, looked like a regular kitchen. Cheerful stripes of yellow, green, and orange vegetables covered the walls. A large table was piled high with newspapers and mail.

"I've never had such a large kitchen to work in," Mom said happily, opening a cupboard lined with glasses.

"Or such a messy one, I bet," Bill apologized. "Listen, I didn't even ask if anybody wants anything to drink. What can I get you?"

We all sat down. Bill bustled around pouring lemonade.

Finally, he took a seat, too. Immediately, he jumped up again, plucking a key ring off a hook near the phone.

"Lucy, dear, before I forget! I had a set of keys made for you."

"How thoughtful," Mom said, then made a funny little groan. "Oh, how am I ever going to keep this many straight?"

Bill reached into his pocket and pulled out his own ring, crammed with keys.

"Here, I'll show you which is which. This silver one is for the front door..."

He laid keys from Mom's ring next to his, matching their patterns and ridges. One of the keys on his chain caught my eye. Copper-colored, it was long and thin with lots of curlicues. It looked old.

"This one is for the basement," Bill droned on. "No, that's the garage."

Out of the corner of my eye, I saw Eric's hand snake across the table and lift up one of Bill's keys. The big copper one.

Bill's hand came down like a hatchet on the tabletop, barely missing Eric's fingertips. His voice was cutting.

"Don't touch my keys!"

I flinched.

My lemonade overshot my mouth and cascaded down my neck.

Chapter Five

"Bill!" Mom exclaimed. "There's no need to shout!" She sounded shocked.

Bill gestured his apology, hands outstretched.

"I'm sorry, Lucy," he said. "I'm not used to children touching things without asking first."

He turned to Eric.

"I'm sorry, son. You know, being part of this family is as much of an adjustment for me as it is for you. Not that that's any excuse for overreacting," he said.

He smiled, dropped his keys in his jacket pocket, and patted it several times. "I guess I'm just nervous," he said.

Mom looked teary with relief.

"Let's just get through showing the rest of the house, Bill," she said. "The kids and I could use some quiet time. You know, jet lag."

"Of course, darling. Britt, do you need a paper towel?"

My neck was sticky but I shook my head.

The dining room and the living room were both large, and lined with formal furniture, such as horsehair sofas and glass-front cabinets. Walking through these two rooms led us back to the entryway.

I couldn't help imagining how weird it would be to live alone in this big, quiet house. Grown-ups are pretty brave, I thought — or maybe just too dumb to get spooked.

Eric pushed past me as we went upstairs.

"I want to see my room first!" he shouted. I ignored him.

The upstairs hall was bright and pretty. The wallpaper looked new. I counted six doors off the hallway. Wow. Six bedrooms.

The stairs came up in the center of the hall. On the left side were four bedrooms. Eric was in one of them with Mom and Bill. Shouts of "Cool!" and "This is great!" erupted every few seconds.

On the right side were two doors, with a long empty wall between them — empty except for a tall dark cabinet with knobby legs. And gargoyles as drawer handles. Jeez, I thought, walking toward the room I suspected was mine — this proves it. Bill has lousy taste.

"Oh, Brittany, you found your bedroom!" Mom called. "Did I describe it well?"

She had done a pretty good job. But nothing could have prepared me for this wallpaper. The room was *encrusted* with roses. Fat pink ones. Bulging out of their tidy wallpaper rows. Darker roses in the bedspread, and still more on the curtains.

Wrought iron roses held back the curtains. The needlepoint cushion in the rocking chair was, of course, a rose. Even the pink and red rug was covered with old dusty-looking roses.

I expected a swarm of bees any minute.

"Well, it sure is different," I said.

Mom laughed. Bill chuckled as he came up behind her.

"Your Mom and I talked about letting you redecorate this room," he said jovially. "I think anything would be an improvement."

"Where are the secret hideouts?" Eric asked.

"Look over here," Mom said, walking towards one of the dormer windows. The two dormers were like cute little hallways, with a window seat and window at each end. I couldn't believe I had two window seats in my bedroom!

Mom crouched low and ran her hand over the wallpaper.

"It's hard to see the doorknobs against this wallpaper," she said.

Then she opened a little rectangular door set in

the wall. Eric and I both cried "Cool!" as we ran over to look inside.

"We need a flashlight," Eric said, peering into the darkness.

"Brittany, you remember where the phone is in the kitchen? The flashlight is in the cabinet right above the phone."

"OK," I said. "Eric, don't look in until I get back."

As I skipped down the stairs, I heard Mom say she was going to lie down for a little bit.

To my surprise, I remembered exactly how to get to the kitchen. I grabbed the flashlight and zoomed back up the stairs, bumping into my bedroom door as I skidded to a stop.

Where was everybody? The door in the dormer was still open. The narrow darkness beyond the door beckoned. I clicked the flashlight on. Then I stopped. Where was Eric?

I stepped back into the hall. Mom's and Bill's door was closed. Napping already?

"Mom?" I called softly.

No answer.

I turned towards Eric's room.

Eric's room was definitely bigger than mine. Big and — at the moment — empty. I went to look in his closet, and threw the door open.

"A-*ha*!" I shouted — at a row of empty hangers. They clanged in the door's breeze. Feeling foolish, I tiptoed back into the hall.

"Eric!" I whispered. The little goon was definitely trying to scare me.

I went back into my room, very quietly. Maybe I could scare *him*. I got down on my knees and threw up the dust ruffle.

Nothing.

I turned the knob on the closet door so slowly it made no sound at all.

Nothing.

I even shone the flashlight into the small dormer closet, expecting his gooney face to leap out with a yell.

He was not there.

Now I was getting spooked.

I crept along the wall into the other dormer to look out the window, keeping my eye on the bedroom door the whole time.

Suddenly I heard an eerie yell rising behind me.

A smothered, desperate sound.

The whole wall seemed to vibrate. My arms flailed.

Then something hard and flat slapped the back of my legs and sent me flying forward against the opposite wall!

Chapter Six

"Aaaagghhh!" I screamed in terror and agony.

My palms thwacked the wall. The back of my calves stung like heck.

Eric's head lolled in the opening to the dormer's closet.

"I can't breathe...I can't breathe in here!"

"Get out of there, you idiot!" I screamed. "You were supposed to wait for me!"

"I was just going to check it out," he whined.

"Look what you did to my legs!"

"Then I wanted to see how dark it was in there with the door closed," he continued.

"Quit lying! You were trying to scare me!" I shot back.

"Uh-uh," Eric shook his head. "I couldn't get the door open in the dark! I knew you'd be mad that I went in by myself, so I was going to wait until you left. I promise!"

"Just get out of my room," I said, pointing to

the door. "You've been bothering me all day, and I'm sick of it. Sick of you!"

Eric climbed clumsily out of the dormer closet. He brushed off his knees. ·

"It's pretty cool in there, but I think there might be spiders," he said. "Also, I would prop the door open when you go in. I almost suffocated."

"I wish," I said. I pushed him out of my room and slammed the door shut.

"Creep," I muttered, as I headed back to the dormer. I had dropped the flashlight when Eric burst forth. Thank goodness it still worked.

I crouched next to the dormer closet, shining the light inside.

"Wow," I whispered, as the beam traveled around the space. A perfect little room. The plywood floor was solid and only a little dusty.

I'm not good at judging how big things are, but I would say the space was about five feet long — just long enough for me to lie down flat — and about three or four feet wide.

Of course, you couldn't stand up in the room. At the tallest point, you could stand on your knees, and the ceiling sloped down until there was barely room for my toes.

Still, I could sleep in it!

I flicked the light around, my mind buzzing with

ideas. This could be my private place. No one else allowed. Except maybe a best friend — if I ever meet one here. I might even decorate it.

I shone the light on the walls. They were made of wooden beams with white stuff in between. I reached out and touched the white stuff. It was hard. I felt sure I could tape things to it.

Finally! I could hang up the posters *I* like!

In our old house, Mom had always insisted on "real" pictures in my bedroom — boring stuff that *she* picked out.

I checked out the other dormer closet. Turned out to be exactly the same. I decided to make that one my hideout, since Eric had gotten into the other one already.

I crawled inside. Kind of a tight fit. Definitely a one-woman hideout.

But there was room for a few things. I'd need my sleeping bag and a pillow — maybe a few pillows to lean against. I could find a box for a table. I'd bring in my little trunk, where I kept all my letters and really private stuff. And, of course, my diary.

It would be cool to have snacks up here. I could see myself, reading for hours — mysteries are my favorites — popping jawbreakers and munching on chips.

I climbed out of the closet, eager to get started.

I had no idea where our packing boxes might

be.

I peeked out my bedroom door. Eric's door was closed, but I heard him talking to himself in a soft voice.

Mom had had an hour to rest, I decided. I tapped softly on her door.

At home, I used to barge right into Mom's room. Somehow I didn't think Bill would be thrilled with that.

"Come in," Mom said. I pushed the door open slowly and looked around.

So this was Mom's new bedroom. Yikes.

The walls were dark green. Heavy curtains hung in the dormer windows. An ornate canopied bed dominated the center of the room.

Beyond the bed stood a lovely dressing table, its tall mirror gleaming in the dim light.

Mom sat before the mirror with her back to me, brushing her dark hair over her shoulder.

I moved towards her.

She raised her head. I felt the hair stand up on my arms.

The eyes that met mine in the mirror were not my mother's.

For an endless moment, those eyes held mine, boring wordlessly into my mind.

Then her pale lips parted.

Chapter Seven

I turned and blundered back through the door. I even said "excuse me" as I closed it!

My mind whirled. I ran to the top of the stairs.

Mom's voice rang out.

"Brittany!" She sounded alarmed.

I was almost afraid to look. Mom stood outside her bedroom door, her hand on the doorknob.

"Sweetie, what's wrong? You looked so strange when you came in."

"Who was that?" I asked, my voice shaky.

Mom came towards me and gave me a hug.

"Who?"

"That woman," I said against her shoulder.

"What woman?" she leaned back, watching my face carefully.

"That woman, Mom! In your bedroom!"

"Just now? That was *me*. *I* was in my bedroom."

"I saw a woman . . . in the mirror."

"Honey, when you knocked on the door, I was sitting in front of the mirror brushing my hair. You came in, looked at me as if you were going to be sick, and stumbled back out. That was me."

"It wasn't you. I know you."

"Britt, the room was dark," Mom said patiently. "I had just gotten up from my nap."

"It wasn't you!" My tone was shrill.

"Maybe you should lie down," she said gently.

"Moomm!" I wailed. Then I took a deep breath. "Would you at least go back in with me?"

She put her arm around my shoulder.

"Of course I will."

She pushed open the door and turned on the overhead light.

"Taa-daa!" she said gaily. "Isn't it hideous?"

I laughed nervously, glancing around. "I think I like it better in the dark."

Mom turned off the light, then gestured towards the dressing table.

"See? That's where I was sitting. It *is* dark in here — your eyes probably took a moment to adjust."

"Mom . . ." I didn't know what to say. That I think I saw a ghost? Or that I'd had a little hallucination?

I wanted to tell her about the locket.

"Mom, something . . ."

She smiled at me. "Yes?"

"Something . . . "

I couldn't say it. She'd think I was crazy. She'd probably be right.

So I finished with the first thing I could think of: "...needs to be done about this wallpaper."

"Isn't it awful?" Mom giggled. "Bill is so adorably old-fashioned."

"It's creepy," I said. "I could never sleep in this room."

"Oh, honey, it's not that bad. This house has a lot of history. I like the fact that it's old. And remember, Bill grew up here. So be polite."

"Are you going to redecorate all the rooms?"

"One thing at a time. Your room first, how about that? Let's talk about what you'd like while I pull together some dinner. I could use your help."

"OK," I said.

We banged on Eric's door as we headed down.

"Eric, come give us a hand with dinner!" Mom called.

"I'm not that hungry, Mom." Eric was never much for meals.

"Well, come down and help anyway."

"All right, I'll be down in a few minutes. Are Aunt Bonnie and Uncle Ian coming tonight?"

"No, honey, they're coming tomorrow night.

Tonight it's just us — our first night in our new house."

I followed Mom down the stairs.

Our first night in our new house. Somehow that didn't sound so good.

Chapter Eight

I snuck a look at my locket while I chopped lettuce.

Faces changing in lockets — or in mirrors, for that matter — seemed completely impossible as I worked in the cheerful kitchen with Mom slicing tomatoes beside me.

And it was.

The pictures in my locket were wonderfully familiar. Mom and Dad. Just like always.

I felt silly with relief. I couldn't stop talking.

"Blue's my favorite color these days, Mom. I read in a magazine that blue is a great color for sleeping. It's peaceful. The magazine said people who like blue are good listeners. Also, we're creative."

"That sounds like you," Mom said. "Do you like wallpaper or paint?"

"Paint, definitely. Can I pick it out?"

"You better. There will be hundreds of blues to choose from

— from nearly white to navy."

"Hmmm, that's going to be hard. I like turquoise, and violet, and light blue."

"Where's Bill?" I asked, reaching for the grated cheese.

"He likes to walk every evening around this time," Mom said. "Tomorrow night I'll probably join him, if you'll keep an eye on Eric."

"Mom," Eric complained as he came into the kitchen. "I can take care of myself."

"I know you can, honey. I guess I really expect you to watch out for each other," Mom said. She tousled Eric's hair.

"Did you find anything to do?"

"There are some old games in my closet," Eric said, and paused. "There aren't many toys here, are there, Mom?"

"I don't think there have been kids in this house since Bill was a boy," she said. "I don't think there are toys."

"Where's all our stuff, Mom?" I asked. "I want to unpack some things."

Mom dried her hands on a tea towel before answering. "I wanted to talk with you about that. Bill and I both think it makes sense to hold off on unpacking until after your rooms are redecorated. Otherwise, everything will be one big dusty jumble."

"Mom, there are a few things I've got to have out of my boxes," I cried. "I can't wait that long! Besides, I can figure out which boxes they're in. I won't make a mess."

Mom looked at me dubiously.

"What 'few things' and how many?"

I hated to list them in front of Eric. He'd know right away what I was doing.

"I'll talk about it with you later, OK?" I said.

"OK," Mom replied. She sounded distracted, and glanced out the window.

"I wonder where Bill is," she said. "It's getting dark."

"I'll go look for him, Mom," I offered.

"All right, honey. You should be able to spot him from the front porch, if he comes back the same way he went. As soon as you see him, give me a yell and I'll put the steaks on."

I went out onto the front porch and sat in one of the metal chairs.

It was peaceful outside.

Birds darted from tree to tree, settling for the night. Crickets filled the air with their gravely calls.

I watched the red rim of the sun disappear over the tops of the trees.

The quiet was amazing. No car sounds. No children playing or dogs barking.

I thought I saw something coming down the road, still a fair distance away. I squinted in the dusky gloom.

The shape was tall and thin. There was no bobbing motion to the walk. It seemed to glide instead.

Every few seconds I lost sight of the shadow, and wondered if I was imagining things.

Then I would see movement against a tree trunk or hedge, and fix my sights on it again.

The shadow turned into the long driveway. It was Bill. His pale face seemed to glow as he strode towards the house.

I kept expecting him to say hello. But his gaze was fixed on something above my head. Maybe that fan-shaped window.

He paused for a moment with his hand on the lamp post. He stared upwards with a weird twisted smile on his face.

I suddenly realized that Bill probably couldn't see me, because my chair was partly hidden behind one of the vine-covered columns. And the porch light wasn't very strong.

"H-hi, Bill," I broke the silence.

Bill recoiled, lurching back.

His face looked ghastly in the lamplight.

Then he lunged forward, making me jump.

"Who's there?" he hissed.

36

Chapter Nine

I leapt out of my chair, sending it clanging against the wall behind me.

"S-sorry, Bill! It's j-just me!" I stammered.

Bill glared at me fiercely.

"I thought you saw me," I lied a little.

"I didn't," Bill said. He continued to stare at me, with a small odd smile on his face. Then his whole body relaxed.

"Nope, I didn't," he said, and smiled broadly. "Come on, kid. We scared each other to death. Let's go tell your Mom all about it."

I ducked under his arm as he held the screen door open. As he walked behind me down the hall, I could feel his eyes boring into the back of my neck.

"Uh, Mom, Bill's here," I said lamely. I sat at the table next to Eric. "Sorry, I forgot to let you know when I saw him."

"What, were you all getting nervous?" Bill asked cheerfully, winking at me.

"No," Mom said happily, wrapping her arms around Bill's waist. "I had this vision of you walking in the front door, greeted by the aroma of sizzling steak and onions — and then coming into the kitchen to a lovely wife and a pretty table with candlelight."

"Well, heh-heh," said Bill, "one out of three ain't bad."

The two of them nuzzled while Eric and I stared at our forks. When I looked up, Eric was staring at me.

"What's wrong?" he whispered.

"Nothing," I said. "I'll tell you later."

I was starving. I let everyone else talk while I put away tons of salad and steak. Mom was particularly chatty.

"I thought I would line up tennis lessons for both of you kids," she said. "You know, morning classes where you're grouped with other kids your age. And, I thought either swim lessons or just joining a pool would be a welcome relief from this heat."

"That sounds pretty good," I said. "Is there a pool near here?"

Bill shrugged. "There used to be a community pool near the library."

"I'll call around tomorrow," Mom interrupted. She turned to Bill. "Honey, what time do you want Ian and Bonnie to come for dinner tomorrow evening? I was thinking it would be nice if they got here early. That'll give us more time to talk."

"Sounds fine to me," replied Bill.

"When can we go to the farmhouse, Mom?" asked Eric eagerly.

"Probably this weekend, honey. Aunt Bonnie and Uncle Ian work during the week, remember. Who wants dessert?"

I was stuffed. But Eric and Bill wanted ice cream. They decided to eat it on the front porch.

"I'm going to make myself a cup of coffee. You boys go on out. Britt and I will bring your ice cream," Mom said.

"Ah, personal service. How nice," said Bill, clapping Eric on the back. "C'mon, son."

I scooped both bowls of ice cream. Mom cleared the table. She was humming.

"Good salad, honey," she said, dropping a kiss on the top of my head. "Today's been a nice day, all things considered. You looked tired at dinner, hmm?"

"I guess. It's going to be kind of weird sleeping in that rose garden of a room."

"You'll be all right. Just keep your lights on."

Mom placed her mug and the bowls on a tray, picked it up, and smiled at me.

"Coming?"

Suddenly, I felt frustrated with her easy solutions and cheery expression.

"No, I want to call Dad," I said coolly. "Tell Bill not to worry. I'll call collect."

Chapter Ten

Well, all my lights were on.

It's hard to say if the roses looked better by sunlight or by lamplight. But I *really* hated them in the dark.

So I turned on all my lights and propped open a book. I decided I would read until I was utterly exhausted. By now I'd been reading so long my elbows hurt.

I couldn't relax. Too many worrisome things had happened that day. Hearing the eerie story about William Beard. Eric hiding in my dormer closet. The woman in the mirror. Bill's face when I spooked him on the porch.

Talking on the phone with Dad had helped. I didn't tell him about the weird stuff. But we talked a long time. Dad was always interested in my descriptions of things, and he asked lots of questions. He told me I was brave and mature, and he was proud of me.

Then he talked to Eric for a while.

After that, we watched a little TV in the library.

Then Mom walked upstairs with us. Bill had brought up our suitcases earlier, and she helped each of us unpack. I hung my four dresses in that big old closet. They looked lonely.

While Mom was in Eric's room, I snuck downstairs to get myself a bowl of ice cream. I passed the library where Bill was sitting in his favorite armchair. His black hair glinted blue in the light of the television. He chuckled at some sitcom as I tiptoed by.

On my return upstairs, I went the other way, through the dark, silent living room. I had grabbed a handful of cookies, in case Eric was hungry.

He was. And he was thirsty. And scared. He came to my room three times before he finally settled down.

I told him he could sleep on the floor in my room if he wanted to.

"That's OK," he said, munching away as he sat on the end of my bed. "Mom might get mad."

"No, she won't," I said.

"Well, I hate to say this, but your room's spookier than mine," Eric answered.

"Oh, thanks a lot," I said. How reassuring.

Finally, he got tired and padded back to his own bed.

I punched up my pillow and rolled over on to

my side. I had borrowed Eric's joke book. It was not my usual reading fare, but I knew better than to read something spine-tingling and shivery on my first night in a new house.

I tried to memorize the punch lines.

It's hard to say when it started. It was that kind of subtle noise — like when your ears ring — that begins slowly and then, suddenly, drowns out everything else.

It began as a gentle sobbing. All very quiet.

Each breath was followed by a long shuddering cry.

It was the saddest sound in the world. It drew you in and made you want to weep until there were no tears left.

I listened for several minutes. The sobs grew louder. I felt my own eyes well up as I slid out of bed.

Poor little guy, I thought. I understand exactly how he feels. It's just that, when you're older, you know that crying doesn't solve anything. You get out of the habit.

I opened my door and glanced around the hall. Mom had left the light on in the stairwell. Her bedroom door was closed. Funny, I hadn't heard Mom and Bill come up.

I pushed Eric's door open, and spoke low.

"Eric? It's me, Britt."

Eric lay on his stomach, his arms folded over his head. The room was warm.

Eric's mouth was open. He inhaled with a cute little snore.

He was fast asleep.

<u>Chapter Eleven</u>

There was no way I was going back to my own room.

I couldn't hear the sobbing anymore. But I knew it was still there. The weeping would surround me if I dared return to the rose room.

I thought about knocking on Mom's door, and telling her everything that had happened today.

But I was too scared to walk back into the hall. Too scared to hear Mom's voice beyond the door, and see another woman's face in the mirror. Too scared to move at all.

I looked around Eric's room, my heart pounding. Gradually, my muscles began to relax. The sound of my brother's breathing, his peaceful face, and damp hair comforted me. It all *felt* normal.

I got Eric's extra quilt and spare pillow. Then I stretched out across the foot of his bed and covered myself with the quilt.

It took a few minutes to warm up the blanket.

Just a few more and I was asleep.

*   *   *

"Hey, what are you doing here?" Eric asked sleepily, prodding me with his foot.

"Quit it," I said, rolling over.

I drifted into another dream.

"Well, I guess this proves it — you're the wimp of the family," Eric said, throwing his pillow at my head.

That woke me up for good. Memories of the night before rushed back. I sat bolt upright. And got another pillow right in the face.

"I'm going to kill you!" I yelled, grabbing for my pillow behind me. I couldn't find the darn thing.

By the time I found it on the floor, Eric had hit me three more times. He leapt off the bed and raced for the door.

I was right behind him, pillow up and ready to strike. We both slid on the wood floor in the hall and skidded toward the stairs. Eric laughed hysterically as he hit the stair landing. I pummeled him all the way down.

Pillow-less, Eric surrendered at the bottom of the stairs, and we went on to the kitchen. We were the first ones awake.

I had two waffles with butter and syrup. Eric had a bowl of cereal. Midway through breakfast, I blurted out what was on my mind.

"Eric, some weird stuff has been happening to me. I'm getting freaked about it."

"Yeah? Like what?" Eric asked, a drop of milk running down his chin.

"Wipe your mouth. And before I tell you, you've got to swear not to laugh. This stuff really happened — at least, it seems like it did. That's the problem. Each time, afterwards, I wonder if I just imagined it."

"Well, what? Tell me one thing."

I decided to start with the sobbing the night before.

"That's easy," Eric said, after I finished describing what I heard. "It was Mom."

"Mom?" I sputtered. "Mom never cries, not like that."

"Remember that night she and Dad told us they were getting a divorce?" Eric asked. "She was crying her head off."

"Yeah," I said doubtfully. I hadn't thought of Mom being the crier. I didn't like the idea.

"That doesn't make sense," I said. "Mom is happy. What has she got to cry about?" I wondered.

"Maybe she's worried about dragging us out

here," Eric said, frowning. "Maybe Bill hurt her feelings, or something. He's kind of . . ."

"Strange," I finished, lowering my voice. "I would hate to make him mad. I already got a taste of it yesterday."

"What happened?" Eric asked.

"When he came back from his walk, and I was waiting for him out on the porch? His face was so white he looked like a ghost. And the whole time he walked towards the house, he was staring up at the roof. With a really creepy smile on his face."

"Yuck," Eric said, with a shiver.

"He never saw me sitting there. And when I said hi, I thought he was going to have a heart attack. He *hissed* at me."

"Hissed? Like a . . . "

"Good morning, kids," Mom said, coming into the kitchen with a smile. "I see you both are finding your way around the kitchen. Did you sleep well?"

I frowned at Eric, warning him to let me talk first.

"I got a little homesick," I said. "So I slept at the end of Eric's bed, but once I fell asleep, I slept well."

"You're my sensitive one," Mom said, squeezing my shoulders. "Whatever it takes to feel comfortable this first week is fine with me. As long as Eric doesn't mind."

"I don't mind," Eric shrugged.

"I think I'll feel fine tonight," I said. I kept my voice light and normal. "How about you, Mom? How did you sleep?"

Mom laughed brightly.

"I'm embarrassed to say, I was so exhausted that I fell asleep in my chair in the library. Bill let me sleep. The TV signal finally woke me up and I came upstairs. It must have been about three in the morning!"

Eric's eyes met mine across the table. They were wide and worried.

Chapter Twelve

Eric and I spent almost the whole day outside. The woods around Bill's house went on for miles and miles. At least that's how it seemed.

We walked down a path into the woods and found a creek. Then we walked back to the house and asked Mom if we could pack a lunch and really explore.

"I guess so," said Mom. "As long as you don't ever leave the creek while you walk. When you get tired of exploring, just turn around and come back the same way you went. The creek will lead you close to home. In fact, I'll find you a scarf. Tie the scarf around a tree trunk at the point where the path ends and you start walking along the creek. OK? Promise?"

We promised. I made sandwiches while Eric packed chips and grapes and cookies, and filled some water bottles. He tied the scarf around his forehead and we set off, promising to be back by four in the afternoon.

Aunt Bonnie and Uncle Ian were coming at five.

*   *   *

By lunch time, it was hot. The air was cooler down by the creek, but we did sweat, though. Eric kept wanting to stop and eat, but I made him wait until we found the perfect spot — a flat rock in the middle of the creek.

We had to take off our shoes to get to it. The water felt delicious running over my feet. By the time I got to the rock, Eric had finished half his sandwich.

After we ate, we lay there like lizards.

I checked my locket while we were there. Outside in the middle of the woods, somehow, it seemed like nothing bad could happen. Sure enough, boring old Mom and Dad smiled back at me.

I told Eric about what had happened with the locket on the plane.

He looked up at me, squinting in the bright sun.

"Are you trying to scare me?" he asked suspiciously.

"No!" I cried. "Really!"

"You better not be," he warned. "If you're trying to be funny, I'll . . . "

"I'm not trying to be funny. You *know* I've

51

never said anything like this before! The only reason I'm telling you is in case more stuff happens. I need witnesses."

"I'm not a witness. I haven't seen anything weird! That's what doesn't make sense. Why is it all happening to you? If it is really happening."

I hate not being believed when I'm telling the truth.

"You don't need to worry. I won't be telling you anything anymore," I said. "Just do me a favor. If, one morning, I don't wake up or I mysteriously disappear, have the decency to tell Mom that I thought something suspicious was going on. Could you do that for me?"

Angrily, I stuffed our trash into the backpack and splashed across the water. I stalked up the bank and began hiking along the creek again.

"Hey, Britt, wait up!" Eric yelled loudly. "Mom said we need to stay together!"

I started to run. Branches thwacked me in the face and brambles caught at my socks. I heard a disgusted "Oh man!" ring out behind me.

I laughed to myself as I jogged along. Eric was really behind me now. I could still hear him. My brother's whine could carry over huge distances.

I stopped running when I got a stitch in my side. I dropped my backpack and tried to walk it out, bending at the waist. I realized we had come to the end of the woods. A few yards ahead, I could see a big field.

Eric came barreling through the trees. When he saw me, he didn't slow down. Instead, he made a growling noise and ran straight at me like a linebacker.

I shrieked and darted behind a tree.

"That's what you get! That's what you get for not believing me!" I screamed.

His face was bright red and furious. "You made me drop my shoe in the creek, stupid! Now I have to hike in it and it's soaked! I'm telling Mom you tried to lose me! You are going to be in trouble!"

I could tell he was serious.

"OK, what do you want?!" I shouted. We kept circling the tree.

"I want to beat you up," he said ferociously.

"I'll let you punch me in the shoulder," I said. "Just once."

"As hard as I want?"

"Yes. But just once."

"You've got to hold still. And no punchbacks."

"No punchbacks." I agreed.

I stopped moving and he came around to my side of the tree. He pulled back his fist and held it, trying to make me flinch. I wasn't too worried. But I had learned over time never to say that it didn't hurt, because he kept punching until it did.

This time it did hurt.

"Ow," I muttered, looking at the red mark. "You're getting strong."

Eric looked gratified.

"I didn't say I didn't believe you," he said. "I just *wondered*."

I nodded towards the field.

"Check it out," I said. "We're out of the woods. I want to go over there and see if it's a field or a farm or what."

Eric glanced at his watch.

"It's almost two o'clock," he fretted. "We'll barely have time to get back as it is. Plus Mom said not to leave the creek."

"Ten minutes," I said. "We'll be able to see the creek as soon as we get back to the trees. I just want to look."

The field was huge. The grass was high and golden, dotted with large spreading trees. I plowed through the tall grass with Eric close behind.

I could see a black fence with gray stones poking up between the posts.

"Oh man," I exclaimed. "It's a graveyard! I love graveyards! Especially old ones."

"Oh no," Eric groaned, stumbling behind me. "You said ten minutes!"

I ignored him. This was a real find. An old cemetery out in the middle of nowhere. I pushed through the gate and counted quickly. Six gravestones. Each one different. The letters were faded on four of the stones, but pretty easy to read on two.

I pushed aside the tall grass covering one stone.

"Hey, look! It says Beard! This is Bill's family. Or was Bill's family."

"Don't be gross," Eric said. "Can you tell who it is?"

"Daphne Daltrey Beard," I read. "Born April 4, 1959. Died July 27, 1967. She was eighteen when she died. Do you think that could be Bill's sister?"

"How should I know?" Eric's voice was antsy. "C'mon, we gotta go."

"All right, just let me read the rest. Real quick. Mary Margaret Grantham Beard, born March 14, 1920, died June 13, 1942. Twenty-two years old. Letitia Rose Maddox Beard, born January 29, 1897 and died October 1, 1917."

"Hurry," Eric begged.

"OK! Cool it! Alma Whitsun Beard, 1847 to 1867!"

I scurried to the gravestone in front of that one.

"Anna Rhinehart Beard — all these are women! — born August 12, 1864 and died December 11, 1892! Wow! That's almost my birthday!"

"I'm going," shouted Eric, slamming the gate. He took off through the grass.

I had to see the last stone. I crouched down. It was hard to read through the moss.

"Louisa Gepplewhite Beard. Beloved wife of William. Born 1844. Died 1862."

I stood up and screamed at the top of my lungs.

"Eric! Wait! I found the wife! The wife of William Beard!"

Eric was nowhere to be seen.

A shadow swept over me.

"Aww-aww!"

I ducked as a hoarse call filled the air.

Something swooped against my shoulder, stabbing me with pain.

I moaned as I fell.

Chapter Thirteen

Eric helped me get home.

Sometimes he could be so nice.

When he heard me scream, he turned around. He told me he saw two large crows fluff their wings and settle on that last gravestone.

I had two large scratches on my shoulder. But at least Eric believed me. And we were only fifteen minutes late getting home. Mom didn't even notice.

"Oh, there you are. Did you have fun? Isn't it beautiful around here?"

She actually looked at us.

"Go take a shower, both of you. Uncle Ian and Aunt Bonnie will be here in about thirty minutes. If you get ready early, go ask Bill if you can help with the grilling."

Eric and I both took our time.

*   *   *

It was great to see Uncle Ian and Aunt Bonnie. Ian has always been my favorite uncle. He was real tall, with reddish hair.

He was the kind of uncle who's always just finished some new adventure. He was a photographer, writer, and animal-lover. Now, he was studying karate. He taught Eric and me some really good kicks.

Aunt Bonnie made great cookies. And she hugged a lot.

"Brittany, look at your profile!" she said. "That retainer has worked wonders. I barely recognized you, you beautiful thing!"

I gave her my happiest smile. Nobody had ever called me beautiful.

At dinner, Aunt Bonnie asked a lot of questions.

"So, Lucy, how did you and Bill meet? It all happened so fast."

"Well, it all started at Amy's wedding," Mom said. "We met at the rehearsal dinner. She sat us next to each other and we talked all night. I thought Bill was so handsome, and we just agreed about everything."

Aunt Bonnie took a sip of iced tea. "Umm-hmm. So . . . "

"So, the next day was Amy's wedding," Mom continued. "Bill and I danced until our feet were sore."

"I was there," Uncle Ian said. "I don't think I

got a word in edgewise."

Mom giggled.

"And Bill came by the next day. And the next. And then I flew home. But by that time, we were both pretty sure that we were in love."

"Really," Aunt Bonnie said quietly. "I've never believed in love at first sight."

"Well, Sis, we had three days." Mom retorted. "And then, we talked on the phone, day after day, hour after hour."

She looked lovingly at Bill.

"Anybody want potatoes?" Bill broke in. He looked lovingly at Mom.

"I have to tell you, Bonnie, Lucy is the loveliest woman I've ever met," he said. "I made it a rule in the past never to date a woman with children, but in Lucy's case I had to make an exception."

He smiled at Bonnie.

"And of course, the kids are great," he said.

"Which reminds me," said Uncle Ian, "when are you guys coming out to the farm?"

"Saturday," said Mom. "We'll spend the whole day."

Uncle Ian leaned forward and whispered, "There's a new family member at the farm. Your Aunt Bonnie went and bought herself a horse."

Mom clapped her hands together.

"You're kidding!" she said. "Bonnie, what fun!"

Everybody started talking at once. Mom's face was glowing. Bill had called her lovely. I hadn't thought of her that way, but I could see what he meant. She had long dark hair that she hadn't cut since she was a child. Her eyes were deep brown and very pretty, with thick black lashes.

Suddenly I realized Aunt Bonnie was trying to get my attention.

"Brittany, honey? Is that a locket you're wearing around your neck? Can I see it? I used to wear one when I was a girl."

I unclasped the locket and handed it across the table. Aunt Bonnie winked at me as she opened it.

"I always kept my boyfriends' pictures in it," she said.

She studied the portraits inside for a few moments. The little crease above her eyes deepened. She snapped the locket shut and gave it back to me.

"That's a great picture of your Dad, honey," she said. She paused. Her eyes were understanding, maybe even a little sad.

"But who is the woman? I don't think I know her."

Chapter Fourteen

My stomach twisted at Aunt Bonnie's question.

"Sh-she's there?" I stammered. It took me several seconds to open the locket myself.

Somehow, I knew what I would see. Mom's face. I looked up at Aunt Bonnie, feeling a mixture of disappointment and relief. At least someone else had seen the strange woman!

I thought fast. What should I say?

"Whoever she is, she's awfully pretty," Aunt Bonnie said. "I bet I know — is it your grandmother? An old picture of your dad's mother?"

Everyone at the table was looking at us. I felt myself getting red. I handed the locket back to Aunt Bonnie.

"It's Mom," I said simply.

Aunt Bonnie was flabbergasted. She got a little red herself. After a few seconds, she glanced at Uncle Ian.

"Not one word. Not one single word out of

you."

Uncle Ian lifted his hands innocently.

"Did I say anything?" he asked.

"Ian's been telling me that I need glasses," Aunt Bonnie said. "I think I just got convinced."

She paused, shaking her head.

"I could have sworn I saw a pretty blonde woman. A stranger. But look. I guess the only question is, glasses or contacts?"

"Glasses, definitely," said Uncle Ian, laughing. "Big thick horn-rimmed ones."

Everyone chuckled. A chill ran through me.

Someone was watching me. I turned slowly to look at Bill, who sat at the head of the table.

He alone was not smiling. His eyes fixed on my face. I had never realized how icy blue they could be.

I swallowed, and returned his stare.

Suddenly Bill's big white teeth flashed into a weird grin.

"May I see the locket, Bonnie?" he asked.

"Sure," she said.

Bill opened the locket and studied the pictures inside. He seemed to spend a long time staring at Dad. Then he closed it and handed it to me.

"Interesting," he said in a low voice. "It's hard to imagine how anyone could mistake your mother for a blonde. It makes one wonder, hmm?"

Chapter Fifteen

I didn't have a chance to talk to Aunt Bonnie alone all evening.

I wasn't too bothered about it. I knew there'd be plenty of time on Saturday. The only thing I wanted to know was what kind of woman she'd seen. If the woman was blond, then it wasn't the one I had seen.

I was pretty sure Aunt Bonnie would find the whole thing as confusing as I did.

Nothing made sense. Why were these faces appearing? Did the women want something? How did the crying fit in? Why did Aunt Bonnie see a stranger's portrait, when no one else did?

I only knew two things. One, I didn't want *him* — Bill — to hear anything about the weird stuff that had happened. Two, I couldn't tell Mom, because she might tell *him*.

I had a plan for tonight. A plan that might at least answer one question. I was going to beg Eric to stay up late with me in my room. I wanted to know if the crying would begin again.

Then I had a horrible thought. What if the weeping started up, and I could hear it, but Eric couldn't?

Later that evening, when I suggested he stay in my room, Eric was not interested.

"After what happened to Aunt Bonnie, you're crazy if you think I'm sleeping in your room!" he said shrilly.

"Not *sleep* in my room," I said. "Stay awake late in my room. To see if you hear the crying too. C'mon, we'll play cards and I'll sneak some snacks up. We'll keep all the lights on — it'll be fun," I said. I even convinced myself.

"There's nothing fun about this!" Eric said. "You know what this means, don't you? *We are living in a haunted house!* That's not fun! That's my worst nightmare!"

We were in the bathroom, supposedly brushing our teeth. Mom and Bill were outside saying good-bye to Aunt Bonnie and Uncle Ian. Eric paced back and forth, ranting.

"When Mom comes up to say good-night, I'm telling her what's going on," he said. "And I'm telling her I hate it here and I want to go home. Nothing like this ever happened at our old house. Maybe we could move back and Bill could live with us there!" He almost shrieked the last words.

"Be quiet!" I whispered. "They might hear you."

I turned on the water.

"Listen!" I said. "I agree with everything you just said. But we don't have any proof that anything's happening. Mom will never believe us. She's not going to move just because we're telling her crazy-sounding stories."

I grabbed Eric by the shoulders.

"That's why it's so important that you do this tonight. Because if *you* hear the crying, then that means Mom should be able to hear it, too. Then all we've got to do is get her to listen."

Eric finally agreed. He went to his room to get the cards. I ran downstairs to get milk and cookies. I also made two sandwiches, just in case we got really hungry.

I kept expecting Mom and Bill to come in. But when I walked softly past the front door to go upstairs, I saw them sitting on the porch steps, holding hands. Perfect, I thought, as I dashed up.

Eric was in his room, waiting. He had gathered a pile of comics, deck of cards, and our backgammon board.

"You go first," he said. "I'm leaving all the lights on in my room."

65

We turned on all the lights in my room, too. We checked everywhere — the big closet, the two dormer closets, behind the curtains, under the bed.

Everything seemed fine.

We sat cross-legged on the bed and I started dealing for gin rummy. I thought I would feel nervous, but I didn't. It was nice to have company.

Mom poked her head in, wondering where Eric was. She didn't seem to mind if we stayed up late.

"We're turning in, kids," she said. "You two keep it quiet."

She kissed us both on the head.

"Wasn't that fun tonight?" she asked. "I'm so excited to live back in my home town. It's been so long since I lived near my big brother and sister."

"G'night, Mom," Eric and I chimed together.

She left. Eric snuck out into the hall and turned the hall light back on. We started our ninth game of gin rummy.

The crying started very low. Probably just a little before midnight.

Eric and I agreed afterwards that it probably began about five minutes before we started paying attention. It started so low and quiet.

I noticed it first. I cocked my head.

"Shhhh. Quiet. Do you hear that?"

Eric stopped talking.

"What? I don't hear anything," he said.

"Wait," I whispered.

The sound was so sad. It was a wail so low it disappeared, but then you could hear a short gasp as the weeper took a breath.

"All right, I heard it. I'm going." Eric said.

"Go get Mom," I whispered. "I'll stay here. I'll be OK."

Eric slipped out of the room. The weeping grew louder.

He was back in a few minutes. I was standing just inside my door.

"I knocked and called, but there was no answer," he said. "Then I tried the door and it was locked. I didn't know what to do!"

"Stand with me, here by the door." I said urgently. "Let's see what happens."

By now, I had noticed at least one other sound added to the wailing. A hiccuping, higher, more hysterical wail.

"Where is it coming from?" Eric asked.

It was hard to say.

When I sat on the bed, I couldn't tell. When I stood by the door, it seemed as though the wailing was coming from the left — either from my closet or maybe from the dormer I had chosen for my hideout.

Eric had had enough. He darted across the hall

to his room.

The sounds were louder, more demanding. It was like a baby crying — you felt like you had to do something, anything to get it to stop.

"Eric, wait!" I shouted. Now it sounded like more people were crying as if their hearts would break.

For some reason, I couldn't move.

My eyes darted around the room. The noise was getting louder. I clapped my hands to my ears. I couldn't take the sadness.

"MOM!" I shouted.

The wails got louder.

"MOM! MOMMY!" I screamed.

The wails grew louder still.

Eric appeared in the doorway. He pulled my arm.

"Come on, Britt! You've got to get out! Mom's not coming! *Come on!*"

I let him pull me into the hall.

He closed my door. The sudden silence was amazing. I couldn't hear a thing.

Then something grabbed my neck.

Chapter Sixteen

I yelped in pain.

The vise on the back of my neck was cold and tight.

I could tell by the look on Eric's face who it was.

Him.

"What in blazes are you two doing?" Bill's voice was icy. He sounded furious. "Have you lost your minds?"

I tried to shake loose. His fingers tightened.

"We got scared," Eric said in a very small voice. His hands were shaking. Nice touch, I thought.

"Oh, you got scared," Bill mimicked in a high voice. "That's too bad."

Blood rushed to my face. I couldn't believe it. After what we'd just been through, he was making fun of us. Making fun of my brother.

I whipped free of his grip, and whirled around to face *him*. My voice was trembling but strong.

"Don't you dare make fun of my brother. Nobody could spend a night in this creepy house and feel safe! The amazing thing is that you could bear to live here alone for so many years!"

Bill's face whitened.

"What are you talking about?"

I was tempted to open the door of my room and let the wailing pour into the hall and swirl around us. But some instinct stopped me.

I stepped next to Eric and put my arm around his shoulder.

"Just leave us alone. Where's Mom? I want to talk to her."

Bill managed to look concerned. What a fake, I thought.

"Your mother is fast asleep. Even all the racket you made didn't wake her. I suggest we leave her out of this. You and Eric get yourselves settled, and go to sleep. We'll discuss your shenanigans in the morning."

Shenanigans!

"B-bill?" Eric said hesitantly.

"Yes?"

"Will you take a look around my room, just to make sure there's nothing there?"

"Yes," Bill said impatiently. He stalked into Eric's room and flung open doors and drawers.

Eric and I stood in a corner of the room together, watching.

"There," Bill said. "Nothing out of the ordinary. Satisfied?"

"You didn't look under the bed," Eric suggested.

Bill rolled his eyes. Flinging back the flaps of his dressing gown, he kneeled to look under the bed. He lifted the dust ruffle and stuck his head underneath.

"Nothing but dust," he reported. Then he coughed, and we heard a muffled curse as he cracked his head on the bed frame.

Slyly, I watched him in the mirror over Eric's dresser. He grimaced as he felt the bump on his head. He took a handkerchief from his pocket, pressed it to his scalp, and looked at it.

"Are you OK?" asked Eric.

"Cripe, I'm bleeding," Bill said angrily. "Hurts like ... "

I didn't hear anymore.

To my horror, the reflection in the mirror had changed.

Bill still stood there, dabbing at his cut.

Behind him, three or four shadowy faces loomed into focus.

They reminded me of photographic negatives, all blacks and whites and grays.

Empty hollows where eyes should be. Gaping

71

mouths, wide with torment or fear.

They crowded around Bill's head and shoulders. It seemed he couldn't see or feel them.

Then I saw a white bony hand steal about his throat!

Chapter Seventeen

I spun around and looked straight at him.

"Bill!" I croaked.

"What is it?" he glanced up. There was nothing behind him.

"Uh, never mind," I mumbled, blushing.

Bill glared at me as he left the room.

"Women!" he said, shaking his head. He closed the bedroom door.

Eric and I looked at each other.

"Phew!" I said.

"Yeah," Eric said weakly. "What are we going to do now?"

I decided not to frighten Eric even more by mentioning the reflections.

"Well, it's one o'clock," I said. "We should try to get some rest. I'll stay awake while you sleep. Then we'll switch."

Fear is exhausting. Eric fell asleep in about eight minutes.

I sat at the end of his bed, wrapped in the quilt. I made a point of not looking in the dresser mirror. I thought about the faces I had seen.

For some reason, I was feeling less afraid, not more.

Some things were starting to make sense. The faces I had seen in the locket and Mom's mirror belonged to a woman — the same woman, I thought. Aunt Bonnie saw another woman.

The faces I had just seen in the mirror were hideous and hard to identify, but something told me they were female. Plus, no man could make sounds like the sobs I'd heard in my room.

Which brought my thoughts to the tiny cemetery Eric and I had found.

Six gravestones. Six women buried — all named Beard. The oldest gravestone apparently belonged to the wife of the first William Beard.

The runaway wife. The thief. The would-be murderer.

The wife who was never found.

According to Bill.

A person didn't have to be a genius to guess that the runaway wife had been found — and punished. And that it was her tortured spirit that haunted this horrible old house. With a few other ghosts as her cheerleaders.

Figuring out the mystery in this house was no longer the problem. I was pretty sure I had the basic facts.

No. I had a new problem.

How were we going to get out of this place?

*   *   *

I woke up the next morning to bright sunlight streaming in the windows. I was still wrapped in the quilt. Guess I had just keeled over with exhaustion.

I slipped off the bed and tiptoed out of Eric's room without waking him. The smell of coffee drifted up from downstairs.

Good. Mom was awake. I wanted to talk to her.

I threw on some clothes and hurried downstairs. I stopped short in the kitchen doorway. Bill was sitting at the table. Mom had begun frying bacon and eggs.

"Well, here's one sleepyhead," she joked as I came in. "Bill was just telling me about your night, dear. It sounds like things got way out of hand."

I didn't look at Bill.

"Yeah, I guess so," I murmured. "Sorry about that, Bill."

"Things look a little different by the light of day, kiddo?" Bill asked.

75

"They sure do," I answered in a smarmy voice. "Eric and I really spooked ourselves."

"It's funny," Mom said. "I have never slept so deeply as I have in this house the last couple of nights. I haven't even had any dreams."

She served Bill a plate heaped with eggs and bacon.

"Now that looks good!" he said, then added with a wolfish smile. "I guess I'll keep you — all of you — after all." He forked a big bite into his mouth.

I shivered. It was hard to imagine I had ever thought Bill was the slightest bit handsome. His wavy black hair and pale blue eyes made him look like an evil magician.

Or worse.

Chapter Eighteen

Mom had big plans for the day.

"Bill, I'm going to take the kids shopping for paint and fabric and a few things to lighten up their rooms," she said. "I really think that's the problem here. Their bedrooms are just too gothic."

"Mom, do I have to go? You can just pick out a color for me," begged Eric.

"Yes, you have to go. It'll do us all good to get out of the house."

"Actually, Lucy, I think I'll join you," Bill said, grabbing his keys and pushing back from the table. "I don't have anything pressing to do today."

"Wonderful!" said Mom. "We'll make a day of it. Kids, run upstairs and get ready. And make sure your beds are made!"

On my way upstairs, I realized why Bill wanted to come with us. He didn't want Eric and me to be alone with Mom. He was afraid to let us talk together. Afraid we might draw some conclusions.

We didn't get back until after lunch. I have to admit I had a great time. I love looking at furniture and pictures and wallpaper. I may even be an interior designer when I grow up. At our old house, I used to rearrange my bedroom furniture every two weeks.

I could *not* make up my mind about what color to paint my bedroom. Even Mom got frustrated with me. Finally I decided on light blue with just a hint of purple. Periwinkle Blue, it was called. I thought it would look great next to the white paint on my windowsills and trim.

Eric decided on gray. He thought that would look cool — and definitely not babyish.

Then we went to a fabric store. Mom is talented with a sewing machine, so we bought many, many yards of cloth. She planned to make curtains for several different rooms. I found what I wanted right away — delicate blue, purple, and yellow flowers on a white background. No roses.

Eric picked a plaid with lots of red and dark green.

While we ate lunch, we talked about redecorating and unpacking and where our belongings could go.

Clouds had been building all day. On the way home in the car, it started to rain. A hard steady rain. I could hardly wait to get to the house, so I could try out my dormer hideout with rain and a good book.

We decided to leave everything in the car trunk until the rain stopped. Eric, Mom, and I dashed in from the car, laughing. Bill parked it in the garage behind the house.

Mom had told me I could unpack my stuff, so I went straight to the parlor, where the boxes were. Fortunately, I had put all my most important stuff in two boxes. And I'd labeled them, so they were easy to find.

I hefted both boxes upstairs to my room. This was fun.

I pulled out my sleeping bag first. Then a couple of pillows — one quilted by my grandma, and another with the slogan "Gotta Love Me." Those definitely would go in the hideout.

I reached in the second box and lifted my trunk out. I knew better than to open it. It always took about two hours to read everything in it, and I didn't have that kind of time.

I unrolled my posters and flattened them with heavy books. It would take at least a day for them to uncurl.

After about thirty minutes, I had my hideout arranged. I crawled in with Bill's flashlight, a box of cereal, and a book I had been saving for a month.

The rain pounded the roof above me.
Nothing and nobody bothered me all afternoon.
It was heaven.

Chapter Nineteen

The rain stopped around five in the afternoon. About an hour later, Mom opened my bedroom door, calling for me.

"Brittany! Britt-a-ny!" She sounded mad.

I stumbled out of my hideout as fast as I could. Mom was shocked to see me emerge from the tiny opening in the wall.

"There you are! I have been yelling for you for the last twenty minutes! Nobody had any idea where you were!" she scolded as she brushed down my clothes.

"I can't believe you've been hiding in there. I looked in your room before, but when I didn't see you, I started calling outside. Even Eric's worried!"

"I didn't hear you," I protested. "Come look at my hideout. It's so great." I'd never been much good at keeping a secret.

Mom peered inside and laughed.

"You are too much," she said. "Most people

would hate a tiny space like this, but not you! You'd probably rather have this for a bedroom!"

I laughed too. She was right. Eric burst in the room.

"There you are! We've been looking all over for you!" he said anxiously.

"Mom just said the exact same thing. Can't a person have a few hours of privacy?" I complained. "What have you guys been doing all this time?"

"Eric helped me move the furniture in his room to get ready for painting," Mom said. "I'm hoping to have his room done this weekend. We'll start yours next week."

She started to leave the room.

"I'm going to unwind by joining Bill on his evening walk," she said. "We may be gone almost an hour, OK?"

Eric immediately started snooping around. He picked one of the books off of a poster.

"What are you doing?" he asked.

"Flattening out my posters."

"I know a faster way to get them flat," Eric said.

"How?" I asked suspiciously.

"You just roll them in the opposite direction a couple of times. I'll show you!"

"No!" I exclaimed. "I'll do it." To my surprise,

it worked pretty well. So we re-rolled them all.

"We might as well hang them now," I said. "Come here. Look what I did to my hideout, Eric."

He peered in.

"Wow. You are *so* lucky. Is this where you were the whole afternoon?"

"Yep. And it was raining, which made it really cozy."

"Can I go in?" Eric asked. "I'll help you hang up your posters."

"You can go in for a few minutes. Then I'll go in and you can hand me the posters. I want to hang them myself."

Hanging my posters didn't take long. After I finished, Eric had a brilliant idea.

"I know what would be really cool, Britt! Hang on! I'll be right back!"

When he returned, he had a handful of nails and a hammer.

"Mom took these nails out of my walls, to get them ready for painting," he said. "I have a great idea for hanging the flashlight, so we don't have to hold it all the time."

I climbed out reluctantly. Eric scrambled in.

As I watched through the door, Eric moved to the opposite wall. Kneeling, he positioned a nail above the poster I'd hung there. Then he picked up the hammer and banged away.

While I watched, the wall collapsed in a cloud of powder.

Eric fell right through.

Chapter Twenty

"Eric!" I screamed.

Total silence.

"Are you OK?" I yelled.

I heard hacking and coughing. Followed by groaning.

"Oh, no. Oh, no. Oh, no. Please don't tell Mom."

Eric raised himself up. His face and hands were white with dust.

"I'm in trouble," he said.

"You messed up my whole hideout," I said.

Then I felt kind of sorry for him.

"Maybe not," I said. "I doubt Mom will look in here again. And I won't tell Bill about this place, ever. Maybe we can fix it."

Eric looked around.

"I'm done for," he said. "We can't fix this."

"See if there are any big pieces of wall we could put back," I said.

"OK," Eric said. He leaned back into the hole

he'd made.

"Britt," he said, "there are no big pieces. But you know what? I can see light up ahead. And there's a floor we can crawl on."

That interested me.

"It's probably Mom's room," I said. "What can you see?"

"It seems like it's too light to be Mom's room. Let's see what it is. It could be like a huge hideout for both of us. C'mon!" Eric said.

I hesitated, thinking about the time.

"Mom and Bill will be back any minute, and I don't want them looking for us," I said.

"As soon as we see what this leads to, we'll turn around. Bring the flashlight."

Eric's voice was getting fainter as he pushed through the hole. White powder swirled around my hideout and coated everything. We'll need to take showers too, I thought, climbing back into the little closet.

I picked up the flashlight and lunged through the hole on my hands and knees. Eric was waiting for me, and for more light.

"Shine it in front of us," he whispered. "See how light it is up ahead? But there's something blocking the light."

We were in a corridor shaped exactly like my

hideout, with a solid floor and a low sloped ceiling. I'd say it was about twenty feet long. We crawled quickly. Like rats tunneling under the roof, I thought with a giggle.

"This looks like a treasure chest," Eric muttered, coming to a halt. A large trunk and two smaller wooden crates prevented us from moving forward. I sat down and hugged my knees, shining the flashlight all around the corridor.

"This is great, Eric," I said. "It'll make a huge hideout."

"Yeah, but don't you want to see what's on the other side of this chest?" Eric was on his knees, peering over the top of the trunk. "It looks like a room, or an attic."

He pushed against the trunk. It barely budged.

"Help me move this, Britt."

"No, we need to go back," I said firmly. "Bill will kill us if he finds out about that hole you made. We'll try it later."

Eric loitered behind a few more seconds, but I had the flashlight.

I let him take the first shower.

*   *   *

I dashed downstairs to the kitchen, my hair still

87

dripping a little. Mom was doling out pizza slices to Bill and Eric. She looked up as I came in.

"Good. I'm glad you each took a shower. Do you want pizza with everything, or just vegetables?"

"Just vegetables, please. Yeah, we were dusty."

I was really quiet at dinner. Thinking.

Night was coming. Our third night in this creepy house.

Part of me wanted to get back to my room, to clean up my hideout. Part of me wanted to beg Mom to stay in my room so she could hear the crying. Part of me wanted to run screaming out the front door and never come back.

Finally, I basically chickened out. I was just too tired, after two almost sleepless nights in a row, to face more scary stuff.

"Mom?"

"Yes, dear?"

"Would it be OK if I slept on the floor in Eric's room? I'll use my sleeping bag."

"Honey, all his furniture's been moved around."

She frowned at my pleading face.

"Oh, I guess so. But listen, don't think for a moment that this arrangement will continue. As soon as your rooms are redecorated, you're just going to have to adjust."

"Thanks, Mom." I got up from the table. "Eric, you have to help me clean up my room. May I please be excused?"

Chapter Twenty-One

Eric helped me clean up. We used paper towels to wipe up the white powder, which I figured must be plaster dust.

"Where are Mom and Bill?" I asked.

"They're sitting on the front porch, probably right below us," Eric said.

"Do you think they can hear us?" I whispered.

"Nah, we're not making much noise," he answered.

"I need to shake the dust out of my sleeping bag and pillows. I guess I'll go outside through the kitchen."

I staggered down to the kitchen, my arms heaped with stuff. As I passed the kitchen table, something glinted and caught my eye. It was the big copper key on Bill's key chain. Unusual to see the key chain by itself. Bill almost always carried it.

I put my armload down on a chair and picked up the keys. The copper key was heavy, and smooth as satin. It looked really old. My finger ran along every fancy curlicue.

I thought I heard a noise behind me. Quickly, I put the keys down exactly where I had found them.

Picking up my sleeping bag and pillows, I pushed through the screen door. It took me about five minutes to shake the powder off everything. By the time I finished it was dark.

*   *   *

Nothing scary happened that night, thank goodness.

Eric and I didn't even set a big toe in my room after nine-thirty, and we made sure my door was closed so we couldn't hear a thing. I slept like a log and woke up in a good mood, feeling refreshed.

My mood got even better when Mom told me Bill had left for the day.

"He had to go into town for business," Mom said. "He'll be gone until this afternoon. So I'm going to use this time to really get some work done in your brother's room. Which means you two need to entertain yourselves for the day."

"Can I help you paint, Mom?" Eric asked.

"No, honey. I've only got one paint roller and I'll go faster if I can just concentrate on what I'm doing," Mom replied.

"Don't worry, Mom. Eric and I will find stuff to do," I said.

I looked at Eric meaningfully. Shut up, my look said. This couldn't be more perfect. Bill's gone. Mom's busy. We're on our own.

A few minutes later, we were huffing and puffing in the corridor, our backs against the side of the trunk, pushing with our feet.

The thing weighed a ton. It moved an inch at a time.

Eric wanted to open the "treasure chest" and there wasn't room to open it in the corridor. I wanted to see what was on the other side of the trunk.

We had been able to slide the two smaller boxes with our feet, out into the space beyond the trunk. I had stretched out alongside the trunk where the boxes had been, trying to see what was there. The boxes still blocked my view. But the light in the space was sunlight. And it wasn't green enough to be Mom's room.

So we pushed the trunk. When we finally muscled it out of the corridor, we just sat there, panting. And looking around.

We were in a small, unfinished room. The walls were plain wood, like in an attic. The room looked like a tiny attic or storage room. It was crammed with furniture and rolled up rugs. The light was coming from a window above us.

The fan-shaped window!

"Look, Eric!" I said. "There's the window you can see from outside, in the front. The one between Mom's dormer windows and mine!"

"I know, I know," Mr. Know-it-all said. "I wondered where that window was. You can see it from the outside, but not on the inside. That's weird!"

I stood up and flexed my legs. My eyes lit on a tall glass cabinet that stood against one wall. Inside it were mounted all kinds of weapons — a beautiful old sword, thin and curved; several hunting knives with wicked-looking blades; a bayonet; and an old hunting rifle.

On the bottom shelf, there were two coils of rope and a row of old glass bottles, unlabeled. Several were filled with powder, the others with liquid.

"No wonder Bill keeps this out of sight," Eric whispered in an awestruck voice. "Do you think the guns are loaded?"

"Probably not," I said, glancing around. Even mentioning Bill's name made me nervous.

Then I saw another surprise. "Eric! A door!"

"Where do you think it goes?"

"I have no idea," I said. The mystery door was opposite the wall with the fan-shaped window. This little attic room was between Mom's and Bill's bedroom and mine. So this door would open into the up-stairs hall?

"I'll try it real slow," I whispered. The crystal and brass doorknob looked like it might break off in my hand. Below it was a large keyhole, set in a copper plate.

I tried to look through the keyhole.

All I could see was darkness.

Very slowly, I gripped the knob and started to turn it.

What if the door opened into Mom's room, and Bill was there because he'd come home early? I shivered at the thought.

Slowly, I turned until the knob could turn no more.

Gently I pulled, hoping the door wouldn't squeak.

It didn't.

To my horror, the doorknob came right out of the door.

And I fell backwards with a loud thump!

Chapter Twenty-Two

Eric was appalled.

"Let's get out of here!" he blurted in a hoarse voice.

"Shhhh!" I warned. "Maybe nobody heard me. Mom's the only one here."

We waited a few minutes. Nothing happened. I got up to check the door.

The crystal doorknob had a bolt on the end that slid neatly back into the hole in the door. But it wasn't attached to anything. There was no doorknob on the other side of the door. When I pulled the slightest bit, it came right out.

I leaned over and peeked through the doorknob hole. Darkness. But I could slide my pinkie finger through.

"Can you feel anything?" Eric asked nervously.

"Sort of. Whatever it is, it's not hard. It could be paper. It kind of gives when I press against it."

I paused, thinking.

"This door must have been locked through the keyhole," I said. WHAT DOES THIS MEAN?

"This is giving me the creeps," Eric said. "I want to go check on Mom. Are you coming?"

"No, I'm going to stay. I'm not scared."

I watched Eric slip behind the trunk, back into the corridor.

"Eric! Don't say a word of this to Mom."

"I won't. Hey, do you want me to make some sandwiches?"

"That would be great." I turned back to look around the room.

I looked in the trunk first. No wonder it was so heavy. The top layer was an odd assortment of shoes, boots, and hats. Some of the boots seemed to be very old. The leather was dry and peeling, and the laces were frayed. I tried on a couple of hats in front of the glass cabinet.

Further down, I found a couple of umbrellas — more like fancy parasols. And an incredibly heavy full-length fur coat. It had been laid between two sheets of coarse paper, and it reeked of moth balls.

Below that there were two beautiful, hand-stitched quilts. Finally, at the bottom, there must have been forty fat old books. They had been placed in rows with their spines showing. I pulled out a musty volume called *Modern Etiquette for Young Ladies.*

On the inside cover, written in pretty cursive, were the words, *"This book belongs to Miss Mary Margaret Grantham. Please return if found."*

One of the ladies in the cemetery, I thought. How sad. I put the book back, stood up, and stretched. What was taking Eric so long?

I walked over to the opposite wall. Two huge wardrobes to choose from. I opened the one on the left.

I gasped when I saw what hung inside. Gorgeous old dresses, dozens of them! Each one prettier than the last. I raked through them.

Then I heard a noise behind me.

Eric was back with the sandwiches. He squeezed from behind the trunk, frowning at the sight of its contents strewn everywhere.

"I hope you don't think I'm helping you put all that stuff back," he said. "Here's your sandwich."

"Thanks," I said. "Did you find Mom?"

"Yeah, she's painting away. I don't think she heard a thing. How much longer are you going to stay in here?"

"I don't know. Why?"

"Uncle Ian called while I was making lunch. He wants to pick us up after work, and take us out to play miniature golf or go bowling or something. He said we could decide."

"That sounds fun. Did Mom say it was OK?" I asked.

"Yeah, but she's got a couple of chores for us before we go. Hey, you know what? I think I figured out where that door might be."

"Where?"

Eric swallowed a bite of sandwich before he answered.

"You know that big old dresser in the hall between your bedroom and Mom's? I bet it covers up the door. That's why the doorknob on the other side was taken off. If it's flat, wallpaper could cover it."

"I'll bet you're right! I *thought* I felt paper on the other side. How weird, though! Why would Bill cover up the door? Why not just keep it locked?" I wondered.

"I have no idea," Eric said. "But the longer we're in here, the more I'm scared we're going to get caught. Bill wouldn't like us snooping around in his private family stuff, I'm positive."

"Did you lock my bedroom door when you came through with the sandwiches?" I asked.

"Yeah."

"All right, then. There's no way Mom can get in to find us. It's going to take me a while to put everything back the way it was. You can wait in my room if you want. If Mom calls us, you call me."

"OK," Eric said. "Hurry."

He crawled into the corridor.

I'll hurry, I thought, right after I look in the second wardrobe. I might even try one of these dresses on!

I opened the second wardrobe with a flourish. Oh, darn, no dresses. Just pictures.

The inside of this wardrobe was totally different from the other one. It had four shelves set behind glass, like some kind of museum case. On each shelf were several objects, laid out in a careful pattern.

I kneeled down to look closely.

A portrait, framed in heavy silver. Something long and dark curled around the bottom of the frame.

"Uggh!" I shuddered, pulling back. Could that be a lock of hair, tied with a ribbon?

And what was that thin white shard, circled by a gold ring?

My eyes flew to the portrait. I leaned even closer, pressing my hands against the glass.

It was an old, old photograph, brown with age, and very faded. It showed a woman sitting in a chair. Masses of hair were piled high on her head. Her lips curved in a soft smile.

Despite the smile, I recognized her — the woman in my locket!

A tall man stood behind her chair. His hand

rested possessively on her shoulder.

His eyes as cold as they had ever been. For over a century now.

I recognized him, too.

It was my stepfather.

Chapter Twenty-Three

I could hardly breathe. My heart pounded so fast my chest hurt.

I scanned each of the portraits in horrid succession.

Each frame was fixed forever in some ghastly arrangement. Coiled by a thick rope of hair — brown, black, or blond.

And draped with a scarf or decorated with a dried rose.

The rings — they were wedding bands! One for each!

My knees buckled.

If those were wedding rings, then the white fragments they circled must be . . .

I blundered back from the wardrobe and yelled into the corridor.

"Eric!" I screamed. "Eric!"

His face appeared through the hole.

"What is it?" He was scared by my tone.

I couldn't speak. I just waved my hand, begging him to come on. He crawled towards me as fast as he could.

"What is it? What is it?" he asked shrilly.

I took a deep breath and tried to get the words out.

"Bones. Those are bones. Finger bones."

I pointed to the woman in the first portrait.

"That's the woman I saw. In my locket! In Mom's mirror!"

My mouth was dry with fear. I grabbed Eric by the shoulders.

"And the man in each picture is *him*! It's *him*!" I said. "It's *Bill*!"

The look on Eric's face stopped me. He pointed upwards, shrieking.

"And that's Mom — in the picture on top! That's our mom!"

It was their wedding day portrait, in front of the courthouse.

I clapped my hand over my mouth.

"Oh no!" I cried. "We've got to stop him! We've got to get out of here!"

I let Eric scramble through the corridor first. I banged my leg badly on the trunk as I followed. We emerged into my dormer and stumbled through my room.

Eric fumbled with the lock and flung my bedroom door open. It smacked the wall.

He darted across the hall. I was close on his heels.

We called Mom as we ran.

Eric's bedroom door was closed.

Then we heard something that froze us in our tracks.

My heart jumped, then sank.

"Hey, anybody here?"

Bill was home.

*　　　*　　　*

I stood stock still. I didn't know what to do. But Eric didn't hesitate for long. He barreled through his bedroom door, shouting for Mom. I heard a loud crash, then an anguished cry of rage.

"Erriicc!" Mom wailed. "How could you!"

Bill came up the steps, two at a time.

"What's going on up here?" he bellowed.

I cowered as he brushed past me. Then I followed him in. I had to help Eric.

It was obvious what had happened. Eric had burst into his room, where Mom was painting. She'd had a ladder and an open can of paint set up right behind the door. When Eric came flying in, he'd knocked over the ladder and the paint can. There was a wide swath of paint on the sheet and splatters on the carpet.

Mom was not hurt, but she was furious.

Bill was white with anger.

"Were you on the ladder?" he yelled.

"No, I heard you drive up and I was just starting to put things away."

She shook her head, her mouth tight.

"Look at this mess!" she said. "Eric, you apologize to Bill right now for being so careless. And you will clean up every drop of this paint before dinner!"

Eric looked terrible. His eyes were brimming with tears. I was terrified that he was going to say the wrong thing.

"I'm really sorry, Bill," he said, like he meant it.

Phew, I thought.

"I'll help Eric clean up, Mom," I said.

"Fine," she snapped. "And don't think for a second that you two are going out with your uncle this evening. You were supposed to be watching Eric, Britt, not chasing him through the house! I'm going downstairs with Bill. You two get to it!"

I followed them into the hall.

"Uh, Mom? Before you go down, could I speak to you privately in my room for a minute?" I mumbled, careful not to look at Bill.

"I suppose so," Mom said, still impatient. She

turned to Bill. "Honey, you go on down. I'll join you in a minute."

"Whatever you do, don't give in to them," said Bill, glaring at me. "You've been letting those kids get away with murder since you got here."

He walked heavily down the stairs.

You're a fine one to talk about murder, I thought.

I closed the door behind Mom and locked it. My heart started pounding again.

"What's going on?" she asked in a tired voice. "What is this about?"

I wasn't sure how to begin. I walked slowly into the dormer. The door to my hideout gaped open. I gestured to it.

"Mom, I have something terrible to tell you. Something really scary. I know you won't believe me if I just tell you. I have to show you. It's in my hideout."

Mom crouched down, looking concerned. She peered inside my hideout, and gasped. Then she looked up at me.

"You are unbelievable! You won't be satisfied until you've destroyed everything in Bill's house!" She was yelling now. "Ever since we got here, you've been complaining about this house. Keeping everyone up at night! Acting weird and unsociable! And now look at this! A big gaping hole in the wall!"

"Mom, no! Wait! There's more than that!"

"There better not be more than that! Or you'll be grounded for a month!"

Mom moved towards the door. I grabbed her arm. She shook me off. Her voice was icy.

"Britt, I'm not going to tell your stepfather about this right now," she said. "He's already disgusted with your behavior. Later, when he takes his walk, I want to talk with you and Eric. Some things are about to change around here."

She began to close the door.

"Mom!" I said desperately. "Bill's been married before! He's . . ."

"Quiet!" Mom blasted me through the cracked door. "That's *enough!*"

She slammed the door.

On the other side, I heard her say, "Unbelievable!"

Chapter Twenty-Four

After Mom left, I cried for a few minutes. Mostly from fear.

I couldn't think straight. I had botched my chance.

As usual, crying really didn't help. I wiped my nose and took a couple of deep breaths.

It was time for a plan.

As long as Bill didn't know that we knew anything, Mom was probably safe. The instant Bill suspected, we were all in horrible danger.

I didn't know exactly when he married each of his brides, but they all died young. So he wasn't married to them long before he did them in.

I could hardly bear to sit in the house another instant. But there was only one way to get away — the car.

And the only way to get Mom in the car was to convince her we were in danger. And the only way to convince her we were in danger was to get her in the attic room.

It would be risky trying to take her there through my dormer hideout. It was a tight squeeze for kids. I wasn't even sure Mom could fit.

I figured I would have to show Mom the room while Bill was not there. Bill was going for his walk soon. Bill also had the only car key.

That started me thinking, and the final piece of a pretty decent plan fell into place.

I didn't have much time.

*   *   *

"Eric!" I whispered, peering into his room. "I need help."

Eric was sitting in the middle of the floor, surrounded by paint-soaked paper towels. He looked miserable.

"What happened?" he asked glumly.

"I don't have time to explain. I have an idea. Come on, in the hall. And no talking! Just do whatever I say."

We tiptoed into the hall and stood in front of the dark cabinet between Mom's bedroom door and mine. If the mystery door opened into the hall, it had to be behind this big ugly thing.

The little gargoyle handles seemed to grin at us.

"We need to move this," I whispered. "It's not that heavy, because there's nothing in it. I'll bet the only reason it's here is to cover the door."

Eric looked at me doubtfully, but said nothing. We inched the cabinet away from the hall, rocking it back and forth. We were sweating like pigs by the time we were done. But we barely made a sound.

I patted the wall.

"Give me your pocket knife," I murmured.

Eric always kept his pocket knife on him. I let him snap it open.

Then I sliced right into the wallpaper. I heard Eric gasp behind me. I had found the edge of the door, so the blade went straight through.

I went down on that side, stopping only at the hinges. Then over to the other side, up and down. A clean satisfying slice.

I felt for the keyhole through the wallpaper, and slashed and scratched until the lock was uncovered.

I handed Eric his pocket knife.

"Good," I said. "Now for part two. You stand guard here. If you hear either Mom or Bill coming upstairs, shove that cabinet back. Even if it makes noise. Just tell them you fell or something."

Eric nodded. He looked sick with nerves, but I knew he'd do what needed to be done. As I passed his bedroom, I grabbed the roll of clean paper towels and a couple of messy ones.

I went downstairs very quietly. I could hear Mom talking in the kitchen. Hopefully to Bill.

There was a little table in the foyer where Mom liked to put her purse. Thank goodness it was there now.

I set down the towels and reached in, feeling for her keys. My heart was racing. Surely Bill would leave for his walk any minute.

When my fingers found cold metal, I almost yanked the keys out. I caught myself and lifted them cautiously. Soundlessly.

I clutched them in my hand, hiding them in a wad of paper towels. I picked up the roll in my other arm and walked to the kitchen.

Bill did not look pleased to see me. He shifted at the table so his back was turned. Perfect.

"I just need to get these paper towels wet," I said to Mom. "Clean-up's going pretty good. We're really sorry about everything."

Standing at the stove, Mom nodded. She still looked angry.

I paused in the doorway. Neither of them looked at me. Bill's jacket hung on a peg just inside the kitchen door. I turned and, without making a sound, dropped Mom's keys into a jacket pocket. At the same time the paint-splattered towels made their mark.

"Oh no!" I shrieked. I whirled to face Mom and Bill. "I got paint on Bill's jacket! I'll fix it! Oh no!"

I pulled Bill's jacket off the peg and ran to the sink. I turned on the water full blast, and stuck the sleeve under the stream for a second.

Then I sank to the floor, wailing like a maniac, "You must hate me! You must hate me!"

I knew the counter blocked Bill's view of me. I prayed my mother wouldn't look at me as I pulled Bill's heavier key chain out, and stuck it under my leg. I made lots of noise to cover any jangling.

I felt the floor shake as Bill walked towards me. I was afraid to look up.

Mom pleaded with him. "Bill, it was an accident! I'll take care of it!"

Bill reached down and yanked the jacket away from me. I cringed.

"I'm sorry," I squeaked.

"I'm going for my walk," he said in a tight, high-pitched voice. "I'm beginning to think I've made a terrible mistake."

He shrugged on his jacket in the hall.

He must have patted his pocket. I heard the jangle of keys.

The front door slammed behind him.

Chapter Twenty-Five

As soon as he left, I grabbed Mom's hand.

"You've got to come upstairs! Eric is hurt!" I lied. Anything to get her up there without an argument.

"What?" Mom ran out of the kitchen. I grabbed the keys under my leg and followed her.

When we rounded the landing, Eric appeared at the top of the stairs. He looked scared and confused. He glanced back and forth between Mom and me.

"Now?" he asked fearfully.

"Are you all right?" Mom cried.

Eric nodded, looking even more confused.

At the top of the stairs, Mom froze. She gave me a terrible look.

"I'm not moving another step until you explain yourself," she said.

I brushed past her, keys in hand. Slipping behind the cabinet, I separated the thin copper key from the rest.

My hands shook and my hair kept falling in my

eyes. Finally, I inserted the key in the lock and turned it. I left it there, just in case.

Then I pushed the door hard. The uncut strip of wallpaper across the top ripped and the door swung open.

I thought I heard a soft sigh as I entered the attic room. Maybe it was Mom gasping at my latest act of destruction.

Eric dragged her towards the room.

"He's going to kill us, Mom!" he cried hysterically. "We've got to get out of here before he gets back!"

She walked in and surveyed the attic room. Suddenly I felt horribly afraid.

"Look, Mom. Look very carefully at each picture. Yours is at the top." I looked at Eric. "Tell her what we think Bill's done. I want to watch for him."

I walked to my room. The light was fading. I crept through the room to one of my dormers, glancing all about. Everything seemed in place. Nothing had been moved.

I heard a sudden cry of grief and anger — Mom, learning the truth.

I edged close to the window. Hidden by the curtain, I peeked out.

He was coming.

He was midway down the drive.

He didn't run. He didn't need to run.

He knew we were here. With nowhere to go.

His face looked upwards, white as a sheet. His fiery eyes seemed to blaze through my window, my curtains. I felt his thoughts: *I know where you are. Why did you think you could get away?*

My feet would not budge. Screams bubbled in my throat, yet I made no sound. I stood frozen in silence, waiting for him to reach the house.

At that moment, I believed I would not survive the hour.

The front door flew open with a crash.

"MY KEY!" Bill screamed inside the door. "WHO DARED TO TAKE MY KEY!"

I heard Mom's and Eric's footsteps running across the hall.

I wanted to be with them. Suddenly my muscles unlocked and I ran towards my bedroom door.

But Bill heard the footsteps too. He was coming up the stairs. I stopped just inside my door, hand over my heart.

Bill muttered to himself as he strode up the second flight. I couldn't just stand there, waiting to be grabbed. I peeked around the door frame. And saw Bill's leg catch on something at the top of the stairs.

He came down like a tree, his hands in front of him.

Eric popped out of his bedroom door and smashed a paint roller down on his head. Mom was right behind Eric with a can of paint. She swung it across Bill's back with all her might. Bill bellowed in pain.

Mom pushed Eric away.

"RUN, ERIC!" She shouted. She looked around frantically. "Find your sister and GO!"

Bill rose, roaring with anger. When Mom swung the paint can again, he blocked it with his arm. Mom backed down the hall, swinging the heavy can, luring Bill away from Eric.

"Another one!" Bill cried, his voice high and whiny. "Another one attempts to betray me! How could you?"

He leapt forward as Mom swung, and pushed her off balance. He grabbed her arm and twisted it horribly. The paint can thudded to the floor.

"I gave you my name. My devotion. A beautiful home. And this is how you repay me!"

He dragged Mom towards the attic room. She struggled to get away.

He brought her face up close to his own. "WELL . . . I . . . DON'T . . . LIKE . . . THAT! I WON'T STAND FOR IT!"

"Kids, *run!*" Mom screamed. "As fast as you can! *Go! Go! Go!*"

I ran to Eric. Screaming and crying, we huddled together. Mom yelled again. "I order you! *Run!*"

Bill pushed Mom up against the cabinet, just outside the attic room. He wrapped one large hand around her throat. With the other, he pulled the copper key out of the lock. With a horrid laugh, he brought the key to his lips and kissed it.

I shivered.

At that moment, I heard a beautiful sound. Uncle Ian's voice.

"Door was open! Where is everybody?"

"UNCLE IAN!" I screamed. "HELP US!"

Uncle Ian dashed up the stairs. He stared at all of us in amazement.

But he didn't say a word. He just sprang forward with his curled hands up near his chin.

With a loud "Kee-yyih!" he thumped Bill with a sidekick to the chest. Bill flew backwards through the door of the attic room.

An eerie cry echoed through the attic room.

Mom sprang forward and grabbed Eric and me.

Uncle Ian pushed us towards the stairs.

"Move! Move!" he shouted. "I'll handle him!!"

I stumbled down the stairs, looking back, afraid for Uncle Ian.

As I looked, I saw that something terrible was happening in the attic room. Dark forms swirled across

116

the ceiling like smoke. Faces appeared and dissolved. Weird noises broke out, terrible cries of pain.

"Uncle Ian!" I said hoarsely. He was frozen at the top of the stairs. Mom and Eric stopped on the landing.

Bill lay flat on his back. Now he could see the gruesome faces too. He tried to get up, but shadowy hands pushed him down.

He was helpless, as if a huge stone lay on his chest. Sweat beaded on his forehead, and his eyes rolled toward us.

He lifted his head.

"Help me," he pleaded in his old voice. "Lucy, don't leave me here."

Vengeful laughter erupted. Bill's face darkened.

"I gave each of you everything you could want," he snarled. "But still you had to know. You had to try the *key!*"

Frenzied faces swirled over him, screaming. Ghostly hands pulled him back from the door to the center of the room as he twisted and called.

The door swung closed.

The key turned in the lock.

Then Uncle Ian said my favorite words in the whole wide world.

"Let's get out of here!"

Chapter Twenty-Six

We never did go back.

Mom grabbed her purse as we raced out the front door. We jumped into Uncle Ian's car and sped away, scattering the crows flocked on the drive.

A week later, Mom sent a moving crew to load up the boxes in the parlor and empty our closets. I sent special instructions asking them to bring back the trunk, book, and posters in my dormer closet. Only one poster was torn.

I found out later that while I was switching the key chains, my genius brother had strung twine across the top of the stairs. The long piece of twine could only be pulled taut from inside his bedroom.

And also that Uncle Ian had never gotten Mom's phone message about canceling our outing that night. He had come straight to Bill's house from work. Thank goodness.

Mom apologized to Eric and me about a hundred times.

She seemed depressed that first week. I gave her lots of hugs. Mostly we let Aunt Bonnie tend to her.

Eric and I had a ball. Aunt Bonnie's horse was wonderful. Uncle Ian taught us how to canter, and trot, and gallop.

It was amazing how safe I felt at the farm. It was as if Bill — the Stepfather — never existed. I couldn't even imagine feeling so scared, so helpless.

Then we found out Dad was flying out. Eric and I didn't exactly tell him what had happened, but he didn't like what he heard. So he took two weeks vacation from work.

His plane was arriving at three o'clock.

Uncle Ian drove us to the airport. I could tell Mom was nervous to see Dad. She looked really pretty, all dressed up and her long hair in a bun. That was Dad's favorite style.

We waited at the airport gate. The plane took forever to unload.

I pulled out my locket. My good-luck charm.

I stood on my tiptoes, trying to spot Dad. Surely that was him, behind the grandmother with the cane. I popped my locket, wanting to compare the picture of Dad with the real thing.

A chill rippled through me. No. Not again.

With a hasty yank, I snapped the locket off my

119

neck, and dropped it into the nearest airport trash receptacle.

That was Dad all right, waving at us from behind the old woman. I surged forward to hug him.

Down in the darkness, I knew, surrounded by paper and cigarette butts, two tiny faces gleamed.

Mom forever young, with her innocent smile.

And opposite her, another face.

Teeth too white. Eyes too blue.

Handsome. Patient.

And waiting.